A STORY OF THE SPACE SHUTTLE DISASTER

by Robert Marsh - illustrated by Marcelo Baez

STONE ARCH BOOKS
MINNEAPOLIS   SAN DIEGO

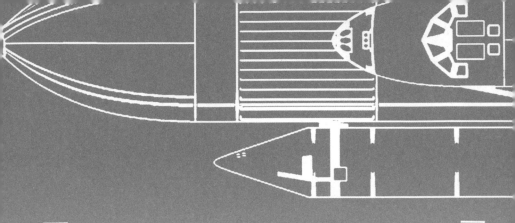

Graphic Flash is published by Stone Arch Books
151 Good Counsel Drive, P.O. Box 669
Mankato, Minnesota 56002
www.stonearchbooks.com

Library of Congress Cataloging-in-Publication Data
Marsh, Robert, 1963–
     After the Challenger: A Story of the Space Shuttle Disaster / by Robert Marsh;
illustrated by Marcelo Baez.
     p. cm. — (Graphic Flash)
     ISBN 978-1-4342-1161-3 (library binding)
     ISBN 978-1-4342-1376-1 (pbk.)
     1. Challenger (Spacecraft)—Accidents—Juvenile fiction. [1. Challenger
(Spacecraft)—Fiction. 2. Fathers and sons—Fiction.] I. Baez, Marcelo, ill. II. Title.
PZ7.M25328Af 2009
[Fic]—dc22   2008032067

Summary: At school in Cocoa Beach, Florida, 15-year-old Dustin Martinez watches
the *Challenger* space shuttle launch. He's always been interested in the space program,
but this launch is even more exciting. For the first time in history, a schoolteacher will
be flying aboard the shuttle.

Creative Director: Heather Kindseth
Designer: Bob Lentz
                    1 2 3 4 5 6 13 12 11 10 09 08

Printed in the United States of America

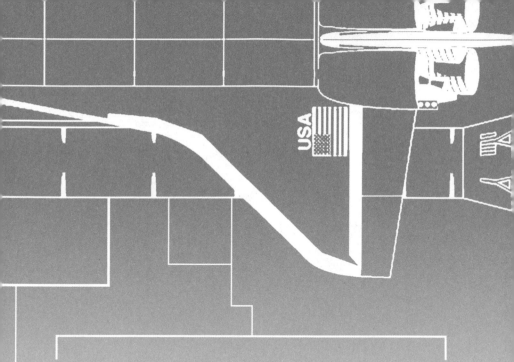

TABLE OF CONTENTS

INTRODUCING...

CHAPTER 1

LIFTOFF!

Dustin O'Malley pulled his headphones off. "It's okay, Dad, " he said. "They're going to push back the space shuttle launch a couple hours."

"Do I look worried?" Gary O'Malley said.

"It got so cold last night a water pipe burst. There are icicles on the launch pad," said Dustin.

"Great," said Gary.

Dustin's mom, Janet, stepped up to the table. It was only seven in the morning and she already had a coffee stain on her waitress uniform.

"You're late," Janet said to Gary.

"They don't have to be at school for another hour," Gary said.

Sam looked at her brother, Dustin, and rolled her eyes. Dustin thought about putting his headphones back on. Their parents were separated, but they argued like they were still married.

"You want breakfast?" Janet asked Gary.

"Do I have time?" he asked.

"Barely," she said, pulling out a notepad and pencil from her pocket. "What can I get you?

"Two eggs over easy, please," Gary said.

Dustin decided to cut the tension. "An *Apollo 13*! Good choice, Dad," said Dustin.

"A what?" he asked, puzzled.

"Two eggs over easy, that's an *Apollo 13*," said Dustin with a smile.

"Since when?" asked his dad.

"Since I became the new manager," said Janet.

"What's so special about this space shuttle launch anyway?" said Gary.

"There's a special hook-up with CNN," Dustin said. "I don't want to miss anything."

"And there's a teacher on board," interrupted Dustin's little sister, Sam.

"Why?" asked his dad.

"She's going to teach lessons from space," explained Dustin.

"But *why*?" said Gary.

Dustin didn't know how to make it any clearer. Wasn't it obvious? "She's the first teacher in space," he said. "Ever."

"Why are you so big on this astronaut thing?" said Gary.

"Who wouldn't want to be an astronaut?" said Dustin. "They name breakfasts after you!"

As Dustin kept an eye on the clock, the students watched reports on TV. They saw footage of Christa McAuliffe's school in Concord, New Hampshire. Her students were ready to cheer for the first teacher in space.

Dustin watched images of the astronauts having their breakfast together. Then he saw the astronauts walking from the hanger to the van that would drive them to the launch pad.

The TV even showed one launch technician handing Christa an apple. Apple for the teacher. She laughed, thanked the man, and asked him to hold on to it. She said she'd eat it when she got back.

The news reporters even had a camera trained on Barbara Morgan, the first runner-up for the Teacher in Space Program. She had trained alongside Christa. Now she was there in the stands, ready to watch her friend become the first teacher in space.

Dustin figured that Barbara wished she were onboard instead of Christa. He wanted to be on board that shuttle too. One day he would. Someday, he'd ride one of those rockets up into orbit. Or maybe up out of orbit and off to another planet or into deep space. Someday, he'd be making history, not just watching it.

He checked his watch — 11:34!

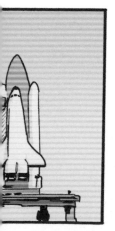

Dustin's hand shot up. Miss Clarkson smiled. "Okay, everybody. Dustin says it's time," she said.

Dustin dashed out of his classroom and into the cold January air. He panicked. A couple kids were headed towards his spot! He sprinted the last few yards and just beat them to it. This was his spot. He always watched morning launches from here. It was away from the building so it had a clear view. It was also higher than the surrounding lawn, so he had a slightly higher view than everybody else.

Dustin pulled his Walkman out and placed the earphones over his ears. He flicked on the radio. Now he could watch the launch and listen to the play by play. Perfect!

It wasn't long before the countdown began. "T-minus twenty-one seconds," the voice from Mission Control relayed over the radio.

There it was! Just coming over the trees. A column of smoke. Reaching up. Straight up.

Dustin's heart soared. He felt like he was up there with them. A moment later, the sound wave came crashing into him. It rippled his clothes and rattled the school windows behind him. His cheeks were frozen, but he could feel them wobble as the sound waves bombarded him.

"Roll program confirmed," said Mission Control. "*Challenger* now heading down range."

Dustin felt the ground shaking beneath his feet. The air roared around him. Go, he thought. Go!

Dustin heard Mission Control in his ears. "Engines are throttling up. Three engines now at 104 percent."

Challenger streaked toward the heavens.

"*Challenger*, go at throttle up," said Mission Control.

"Roger, go at throttle up," said a voice in Dustin's ear. He realized it was Dick Scobee, *Challenger's* commander. Someday, I'll be the commander, thought Dustin. Someday that will be me up there.

And then it happened. There was a flash of light and then nothing but static in his ear.

The roar cut off suddenly — as if someone had hit the mute button. It was replaced by an eerie silence. The wind blew. Thunder rumbled and echoed. Only it wasn't thunder. It came from the white cloud that used to be *Challenger*.

The shock waves stopped. "What happened?" someone asked.

"That's not right," said somebody else. "It's not supposed to do that."

The teachers all looked stunned. "Come on, kids," said Miss Clarkson. "Let's go inside."

Students started dragging themselves back to their rooms. But Dustin didn't move. He stood there, searching the sky for some sign of *Challenger*. All he saw were strands of debris falling, leaving white trails in the sky.

"Obviously, a major malfunction," said a voice in Dustin's ears. It was Mission Control.

Miss Clarkson appeared beside him. "Come on, Dustin. Let's go in."

"I want to stay here," he said.

Miss Clarkson caught the eye of another teacher headed in. "Will you keep an eye on my class?" she said.

The teacher nodded and followed the students inside.

Dustin turned off his Walkman and pulled the earphones off his head. Then he stood still on his mound and watched *Challenger* rain from the sky. He was cold on the outside, numb inside. He hardly felt it when Sam stepped up beside him and took his hand. He didn't feel Miss Clarkson standing on the other side of him with her arm over his shoulder. And he didn't feel the tear that trickled down his frozen cheek.

CHAPTER 2

RECOVERY

Dustin shut the short-wave radio off in disgust. His dad had given him the radio so he and Sam could keep in touch when his dad was out on the scallop boat. That hadn't been very often lately. Dustin was hoping he could put it to use by listening in on transmissions from the *Challenger's* recovery operation.

But the operation's frequencies were a secret. It was like trying to guess the winning lottery numbers. It was pointless.

The room went quiet. The sound of the manatees puffing as they surfaced for air floated in through the seaside window.

"Thanks for turning off that thing," said Sam.

Dustin joined her at the window. Sam kept the binoculars to her eyes.

"I see Rosie, but I don't see Stig," she said. Sam watched over the manatees like they were her kids. Not only did she name them, but she had filled a shelf full of notebooks with detailed entries about their daily behavior.

"Maybe they're getting a divorce, too," said Dustin.

"Ha, ha," said Sam. But she wasn't laughing.

Speaking of their parents, Dustin suddenly thought he heard them.

"Did you hear that?" Dustin said.

"What?" said Sam.

"Listen," said Dustin.

He definitely heard their mom and dad. Their voices drifted in through another open window.

Dustin knew where he hoped to go. But he couldn't waste time blabbing about it. He ran.

"Didn't your parents teach you it isn't polite to eavesdrop?" said Gary.

"Good one, Dad," Dustin said.

"Sorry, but you've got school, sport," said Gary.

"I could call in sick," Dustin replied.

"Your mom would kill me. And I really want to live long enough to cash that NASA check," said Gary. He shook his head. "Sorry, Dustin."

Dustin took a deep breath and acted like he understood. "That's okay," he said. "What time are you casting off?"

"In the morning, about 4:30," Gary said. "I'll be back around 9 or 10 tomorrow night. We could have a late dinner, and I'll tell you all about it."

Dustin nodded and stepped away from the car. He let his dad drive away. But there was no way he was letting his dad go out to sea without him.

Where are you going?

-28-

CHAPTER 3

THE MISSION

Dustin didn't need to tell Sam anything. She already knew the whole story.

"Dad said you couldn't go," she said.

"That's the beauty of being a stowaway, Sam," said Dustin. "You don't need permission."

"I'm going with you," she said.

"No way," Dustin replied.

"I'm the one who wants to be a marine biologist," she said. "If one of us is going to hide on Dad's boat, it should be me. Besides, if you don't take me, I'm telling," she said.

Dustin knew she wasn't kidding. "How long will it take you to pack?" he asked.

Dustin pulled aside a duffle bag and made a space for Sam. "You sit there," he said. She sat in the space and Dustin piled up supplies around her. He then made a place for himself on the other side of the small closet. He stepped into his hiding spot and pulled the door shut.

"Yikes," said Sam. "It's dark."

"Do you want a night light?" said Dustin.

"Guess not," she said softly.

Dustin moved supplies around so he was hidden too. He squirmed back and forth, trying to get comfortable. But he couldn't. There was a rope jabbing into his back. He shifted his legs.

"Ow!" said Sam.

"Sorry," said Dustin

There really wasn't much room in the closet. But at least they were pretty well hidden.

"Now we wait," Dustin said.

"How long?" said Sam.

Dustin shrugged his shoulders. Then he realized Sam couldn't see him in the dark. "A while," he said. "We can't come out until we're at least an hour out to sea. Otherwise, Dad will just turn around and take us back to shore."

"Can I sleep?" said Sam.

"As long as you don't snore," he said.

Sam kicked him. "I don't snore!"

"Whatever you say," said Dustin. "Just try and get some sleep."

Dustin didn't think he'd be able to rest. He was too wound up. Ten minutes later, he heard Sam snoring. He thought about kicking her and waking her up. But since he could barely hear her he figured they were safe.

Dustin rested his head against the wall. He closed his eyes.

Wham! Dustin woke up with a jerk. The ship had lurched suddenly beneath him. He was still drowsy from sleep and couldn't see anything in the dark. But he heard plenty.

He heard the sound of the engines rumbling as they labored in reverse. He heard the slap of the waves as the ship wobbled from side to side. And he heard the muffled voices of his dad's crew.

They were casting off. *Perfect,* he thought. Now if we can just stay out of sight for at least another hour.

Dustin heard another sound. The gentle rhythm of his sister's breathing. It made him realize how sleepy he was. He closed his eyes and immediately nodded off again.

Dustin awoke to the sound of Sam gagging. "I feel sick," she screamed. "I think I'm going to — "

"Not in here!" cried Dustin.

Dustin shoved aside the tarp and scrambled for the door. There was a flash of bright light as the door flew open. He saw Sam dash out into the light. Dustin started after her, but tripped on some ropes. He kicked them off and ran after Sam.

Sam was leaning over the port side of the ship. He could hear her throwing up into the waves.

And what waves! They were enormous and angry. The ocean was a frothy mass of swirling gray. The ship was bouncing up and down like a hyperactive puppy. With each bounce, a spray of mist spread up and over the ship.

Dustin started towards Sam. Just as he did, the ship bounced again, hard. Dustin's feet slipped out from under him.

Without thinking, Dustin jumped up and grabbed the life preserver off the wall. He shoved one arm and his head through the middle of the life preserver and raced for the railing. He pulled at the preserver's rope as he ran.

"Man overboard!" he yelled.

Dustin's dad skittered into the opening of the wheelhouse door. "Dustin! Wait!" Gary said.

Dustin was jolted by the shock of the cold water. It smashed against his skull and raced through his bones like a freezing bolt of lightning. He was so cold he didn't even feel wet.

Dustin jerked to the surface and looked around.

The ship was bouncing up and down about twenty feet away. The crew were scrambling over the deck. Gray waves leapt all around him.

He didn't see Sam.

The water sucked him down one side of a wave then pulled him over another. A wall of water smashed overhead and blotted everything out. A second later, Dustin was back on the surface, gasping for air.

"Sam!" Dustin yelled.

"Over there!" came a voice.

Dustin's lungs ached. A huge wave had pulled him down. For a moment, he wasn't sure which way was up anymore.

Finally, he surfaced. He took a deep breath. Suddenly, something slammed into his back. Dustin instantly remembered that these were shark-infested waters.

His heart hammered in his chest. He turned around, certain he was about to see an open mouth full of teeth chomping down on him. But in this water, all he could see was a dark shape.

It sped towards him again. He couldn't get out of the way. *BAM!* It slammed into him. Part of it reached out and wrapped around his face. It felt like soaking wet cloth. Dustin grabbed at it.

It was Sam's sweatshirt. He yanked at the sweatshirt, and Sam came tumbling into his open arms.

Dustin pulled the preserver off and shoved it down over Sam's head. He then laced one of his arms through the rope that wrapped all the way around the preserver. With his other arm, he waved for the crew. Then he held onto Sam.

The rope pulled tight, and he felt the steady tugs as the crew pulled them toward the ship. Each tug pulled them closer toward safety, and toward warmth.

Dustin watched his dad and waited. He'd never seen his father's hands shake before. His own hands were shaking, but that was from the cold — a cold that was slowly beginning to leave his body.

Back on the ship, he sat there and stared back at his dad. He listened to the ship creaking and water slamming against the hull. Dustin and his dad both looked over at Sam. She broke the silence by taking a slurp of hot chocolate. Sam looked up and saw them staring at her.

"Sorry," she said.

"You could have been killed," said Gary. "Both of you." He put his shaking hands under the table. "What were you thinking?"

Dustin shrugged. He really didn't know. He hadn't been thinking anything. He had seen Sam vanish into the water and he just acted.

"What will I tell your mother?" said Gary.

"You could tell her we're both safe," said Dustin.

"It's the truth," said Sam.

"Barely," said Gary. He ran a jittery hand through his hair. "You aren't even supposed to be onboard."

The ship shuddered as it hit a series of waves. The engines whined. Water sprayed against the cabin windows.

"I guess I'd better get on the radio," said Gary. "Let your mother know where you are. And that you'll be a little late."

He was just starting to get up when the door squeaked open. Rick, the first mate, stepped into the room.

"Skipper, you'd better come see this," said Rick. "We've got something big."

CHAPTER 4

GOING HOME

Dustin looked at the page again. He followed the instructions word for word. He could hardly believe they had found it — a piece of the *Challenger* Space Shuttle.

"Roger that," came the voice over the radio. "Note your coordinates and report in port at 21 hundred. Over."

"Roger," said Dustin. "Out."

He handed his father the microphone who put it gently back in its cradle.

"Now what?" said Dustin.

Gary put his arm around his son. "Now we take it home."

The Navy man nodded. "Good man," he said. Then he and his companion turned and walked away.

A car pulled up at the end of the pier. Its lights spilled across them briefly, then shut off. Dustin's mom stepped out of the car.

"You two stay here," said Gary. "I'll handle this."

"Come on, kids. Get in the car," said Gary. "We're going home."

Gary held the passenger door for Janet while Dustin held the back door for Sam. The women climbed in, and Dustin and Gary shut the doors.

As they rounded the back of the car, Dustin grabbed his dad and whispered, "What'd you tell Mom?"

Gary leaned down and whispered back, "We're under orders to never talk about this, remember? With anyone. Ever."

Dustin nodded. "But — "

"No buts," his dad said. Gary straightened up. "If you're going to work for NASA someday, you'd better get used to following orders."

Dustin smiled. "Yes, sir."

He climbed in beside Sam.

Looking out the window, he watched the NASA and Navy men get in their truck and drive off. He turned back to see his mother watching him.

"You guys okay?" she asked.

Dustin nodded. "Yeah, Mom. We're good."

His head jostled against the seat as his dad turned the car around and headed for home. Out his window, he watched the Navy truck drive off in the opposite direction.

Then Dustin realized it wasn't really headed in an opposite direction at all. That Navy truck was headed the same place he was. It was taking a piece of the *Challenger* home.

ABOUT THE AUTHOR

Robert Marsh grew up in Omaha, but longed to live somewhere else. He pretended he didn't live in Omaha by reading lots and lots of comics and books. He went to the library every week and checked out twenty books at a time. Since he didn't have time to read all those books before they were due, he would read the first chapter of each book then make up the rest of the story in his head. Robert now makes up stories for a living. He doesn't live in Omaha. He lives somewhere else. Dreams do come true.

ABOUT THE ILLUSTRATOR

Marcelo Baez is a professional illustrator and designer who has worked for international clients such as Microsoft, *ESPN Magazine*, *Dallas Observer*, *The Weekend Australian Magazine,* and many others. He lives with his sweet wife and two nutty cats.

GLOSSARY

debris (duh-BREE)—scattered pieces of something that has been broken or destroyed

dredge (DREJ)—to scrape and search for materials on the bottom of a river or harbor

frequencies (FREE-kwun-seez)—the numbers of cycles per second of radio waves

infested (in-FESS-tid)—full of animal or insect pests

malfunction (mal-FUHNGK-shuhn)—when something fails to work properly

orbit (OR-bit)—to travel around a planet

relayed (REE-layd)—passed a message to someone else

stowaway (STOH-uh-way)—someone who hides in a ship or other vehicle to avoid paying fare

tension (TEN-shuhn)—nervousness and worry, or difficulty and strain

wreckage (REK-ij)—broken parts or debris lying around after something has been destroyed

MORE ABOUT THE CHALLENGER DISASTER

On January 28, 1986, a NASA space shuttle named *Challenger* broke apart 73 seconds after liftoff, destroying the ship and killing all seven crew members.

A group of scientists and pilots, named the Rogers Commission, was created to determine the cause of the disaster. After several months, they determined that the accident was caused by a failure in the ship's O-rings, which seal off the ship from its rocket boosters. The rocket boosters use fuel from the fuel tanks to propel the shuttle upward into space. The O-rings play an important role in controlling the blast.

Things didn't go according to plan when the *Challenger* lifted off. High winds shook the shuttle. Soon after, puffs of dark smoke came out of the shuttle's right rocket booster. The heat of the rocket boosters caused the metal casing of the booster to expand like a balloon, which created a hole between some of its metal parts. Hot gases shot out of the hole and made contact with the fuel tank.

Normally, the O-rings would still be able to seal the ship and prevent any damage from occurring when the hot gases came out. However, the morning of the flight was quite cold, which caused the O-rings to harden and lose their flexibility. The O-rings couldn't expand and seal off the gas like they normally did. The heat passed through the seal and burnt a hole in the fuel tank. The fuel and hot gas mixed to create a giant fireball. The extreme force caused by the fireball — the same force used to propel the ship up into space — caused the shuttle to tear itself apart at the seams.

Three days after the disaster, a memorial service was held to honor the seven crew members who died. Over 6,000 NASA employees and more than 4,000 others attended. The astronauts are now known as "The *Challenger* Seven," in honor of their contributions to NASA and our country.

DISCUSSION QUESTIONS

1. Dustin and his classmates watched the launch and the aftermath live from their schoolyard. Many other American students watched it on television. How would the two experiences differ?

2. Do you think seeing the disaster had an impact on Dustin's ideas about astronauts?

3. Do you agree with Dustin's decision to sneak onto his dad's boat? Why or why not?

WRITING PROMPTS

1. Think about Christa McAuliffe, the teacher who was part of the *Challenger* mission. Imagine what it was like for her to receive her astronaut training. Write a story from her perspective.

2. Dustin imagined that he would one day be making history as an astronaut. Write a story featuring an adult Dustin and his NASA adventure.

3. Pretend you are the author and write one more chapter to the book. What happens to Dustin and his family?

INTERNET SITES

Do you want to know more about subjects related to this book? Or are you interested in learning about other topics? Then check out FactHound, a fun, easy way to find Internet sites.

Our investigative staff has already sniffed out great sites for you!

Here's how to use FactHound:

1. Visit *www.facthound.com*

2. Select your grade level.

3. To learn more about subjects related to this book, type in the book's ISBN number: **9781434211613**.

4. Click the **Fetch It** button.

FactHound will fetch the best Internet sites for you.